Disney
PRINCESS
CRAFTS

3 5 7 9 10 8 6 4 2
ISBN: 0-7868-3268-1
LC: 00-110198
Designed by Angela Corbo Gier and Cathy Colbert
Cover photo art directed by Dorit Radandt
Stylists: Jessica Hastreiter and Angela Chan
For more Disney Press fun, visit www.disneybooks.com

Disney
PRINCESS
CRAFTS

by Laura Torres

Crafts photography by Dan and Sherri Haab

Cover photography by Steve Dolce

Disney
PRESS

New York

CONTENTS

❧ INTRODUCTION ❧

Castles, royal balls, a touch of magic . . . nothing captures a girl's imagination like Disney princesses. This book brings those dreams a little closer with some hands-on creativity.

Whether you are dreaming up a ball gown, decorating a crown, or wishing upon a glittery star, you'll find something to inspire your imagination. Enter the enchanted worlds of Cinderella, Ariel, Aurora, Snow White, Belle, and Jasmine with these crafts fit for a princess like you!

These crafts were created for children aged three and up to enjoy with their parents.

Cinderella

Bubbly Bubbles

Cinderella's days were filled with mopping and scrubbing. Here's some soapy fun instead!

Directions:

1. To make bubble solution, measure the water, dishwashing liquid, and corn syrup into the container. Stir gently to mix.

2. To make a bubble wand, ask an adult to help you bend the paper clip into a shape like a circle or heart. Leave a little tail.

3. Tape the tail to an unsharpened pencil. You may want to use a colorful or sparkly pencil. Decorate the pencil with star stickers. Use the wand to blow beautiful bubbles!

Supplies:

3 cups water

1 cup dishwashing liquid

$\frac{1}{3}$ cup corn syrup

Container with a lid

Large plastic-coated paper clip

Unsharpened pencil

Tape

Star stickers

Nice Mice

Cinderella loved to dress up her little mice friends. Tie a merry bow on the tails or ears of these friendly mice!

Directions:

1. Mix the flour and salt together in the bowl. Add the water and stir. Knead the dough until it's smooth.

2. For each mouse, make a small ball of aluminum foil, about the size of a marble. Cover the ball with dough. Dip your finger in water and rub over creases to smooth the dough.

3. Pinch one end to make a face. To make ears, attach flattened balls of dough to head with a little water. Add a small ball of dough for the nose. Cut a few pieces of wire with the fingernail clippers and poke into the sides of nose for whiskers. Stick in a long piece of wire for a tail.

4. Ask an adult to bake the mice on a baking sheet at 275° for about an hour, until the dough is dry. Let cool.

5. Paint the nose and eyes. Let dry. Paint entire mouse with Mod Podge or sealer. Add a ribbon bow.

Supplies:

1 cup all-purpose flour

½ cup salt

½ cup cold water

Measuring cups

Large bowl

Spoon

Aluminum foil

Wire

Fingernail clippers

Baking sheet

Acrylic paint

Paintbrush

Mod Podge glue or acrylic sealer

Ribbon

Lucifer

Keep this sneaky cat that gave Cinderella so much trouble away from your mice friends!

Directions:

1. To make the tail, glue four of the small black pom-poms together. Set aside to dry.

2. To make the face, glue the two white pom-poms onto the medium black pom-pom for cheeks, add the tiny pink pom-pom for the nose, and two of the small black pom-poms for the ears. Glue on the googly eyes. Set aside to dry.

3. Glue four small black pom-poms onto the large black pom-pom for feet.

4. Glue the tail and the head onto the body. Let dry. Meow!

Supplies:

1 large, 1 medium, and 10 small black pom-poms

2 small white pom-poms

1 tiny pink pom-pom

Craft glue

Googly eyes

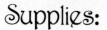

Supplies:

Beads or rhinestones

Glue

Flat button with a loop
on the back

Pipe cleaner

Fingernail clippers

Sparkly Rings

Every princess needs plenty of jewels and gems.

Directions:

1. Glue rhinestones onto the button. Let dry.

2. Stick the pipe cleaner through the loop on the button.

3. Wrap pipe cleaner around your finger to make a ring
   that fits. Twist the ends together to hold the ring in place.
   Clip off the extra pipe cleaner with the fingernail clippers.
   Tuck any pointy pipe cleaner ends into the button loop.

Glittery Stars

Cinderella fell in love with her prince under the light of the stars on the palace grounds. Here are some window star stickers for you to wish upon.

Directions:

1. Squeeze the glue in a star outline onto the waxed paper. Make sure the glue is thick and there are no gaps in the line.

2. Sprinkle on glitter. Shake off excess.

3. Let dry overnight. Peel off stars and stick to your window or any glass surface.

Supplies:
Craft glue
Waxed paper
Glitter

Supplies:

Plastic headband

1 yard tulle

Star wire

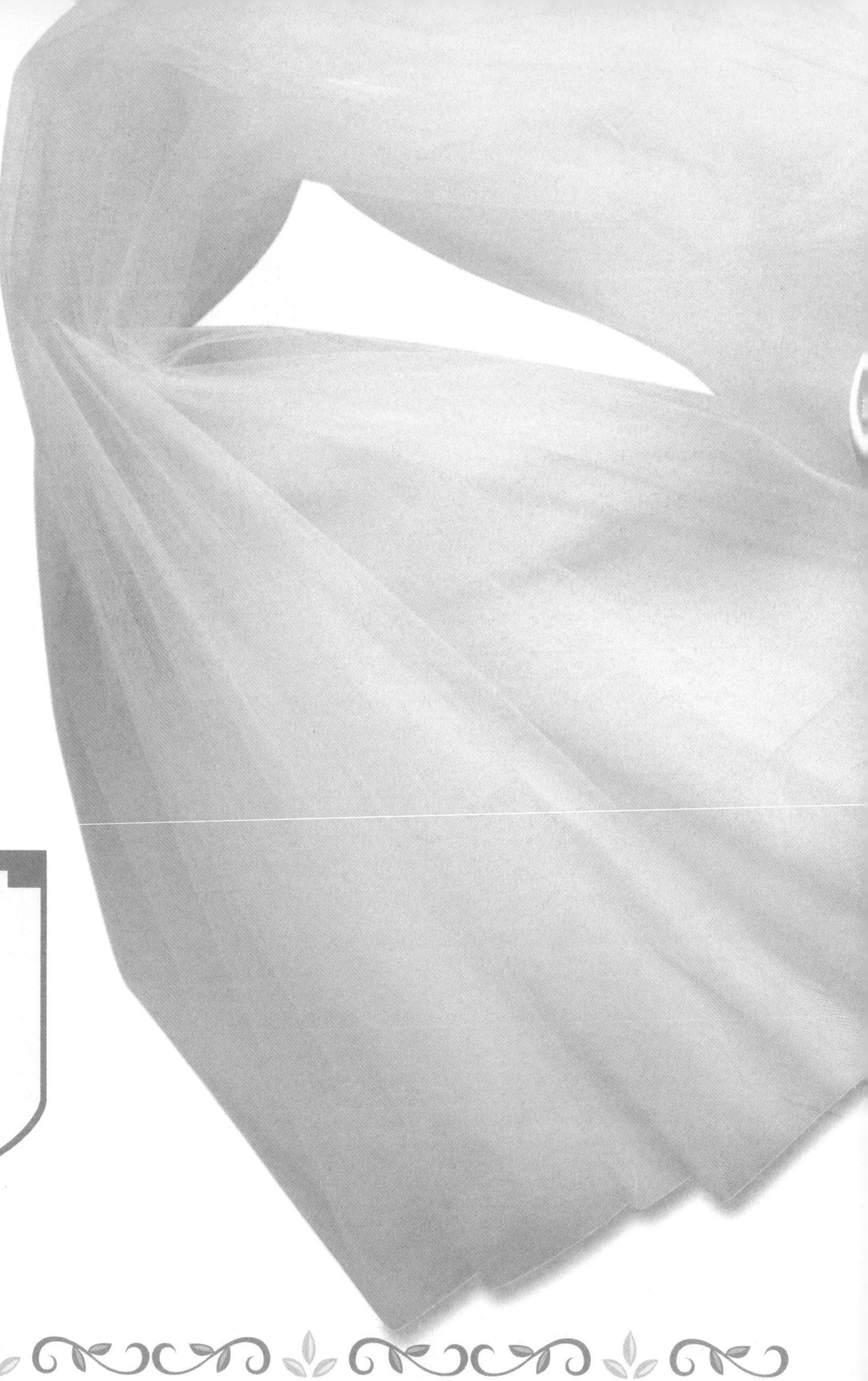

Starry Veil

Cinderella thought her veil (and her prince) were just charming.

Directions:

1. Fold the tulle in thirds the long way.

2. Place the headband on the fabric, about six inches from one end. Fold the short end of the fabric over the top of the headband.

3. Wrap star wire around both layers of fabric, close to the headband to hold the headband in place.

Bridal Bouquet

You can't marry a prince without a beautiful bouquet of flowers!

Directions:

1. Wrap a rubber band around the stems of the flowers to hold them together in a bouquet.

2. Cut from the edge of the doily to the center. Then cut out a small circle in the middle of the doily.

3. Slip the flowers into the center of the doily. Overlap the edges of doily to form a slight cone around the flowers. Tape in place. For dewdrops, squeeze on droplets of glue. Let dry.

Supplies:
Artificial flowers
Rubber band
Doily
Scissors
Tape
White glue

Ariel

Sticky Fish

Create an ocean scene on any glass surface with Ariel's colorful fish friends!

Directions:

1. For each color, measure ½ cup glue and 1 tablespoon paint into the cup. Stir with the spoon until the glue and paint are all mixed together. (Wash the measuring cup and spoons right away when you're finished!)

2. Pour the glue paint into the empty squeeze bottles.

3. Squeeze simple fish designs onto the waxed paper, making sure you connect all the lines. Let dry overnight.

4. Gently peel the fish from the waxed paper and press onto your window or any other glass surface. They will cling to the glass.

Supplies:

Measuring cup and spoon
White glue
Acrylic paint
Paper cup
Plastic spoon
Empty squeeze bottles (you can wash out old mustard or ketchup bottles)
Waxed paper

Trinket Box

Do you have a collection of wonderful things like Ariel's? Here's a place to store it!

Directions:

1. Glue treasures onto the box lid and let dry.

2. Decorate the box with fabric paint, let dry, and fill!

Sea Treasure Bracelet

Your friends will never guess that this charming bracelet is made from fishing swivels!

Directions:

1. Thread beads and charms on fishing swivels.
   (Fishing swivels can be found in sporting goods stores.)

2. Connect swivels end to end and wear!

Supplies:

Fishing swivels
Beads
Charms

Sea Salts

Beautiful mermaids like Ariel live in the salty ocean. You can soak in these bath salts to soften and scent your skin, even if you aren't a mermaid!

Directions:

1. Put a handful of Epsom salts in the plastic bag. Add three drops of food coloring and three drops of perfume or essential oil.

2. Seal the bag and shake until the salt is colored evenly.

3. Pour salt into the jar and put on the lid. Tie with a pretty ribbon.

4. Sprinkle a spoonful in the running water when you fill your bath. Use within two weeks.

Supplies:

Epsom salts
Plastic bag with a seal
Food coloring
Perfume or essential oil
Jar with a lid
Ribbon

Ocean Beauty Ornament

Natural gifts from the sea make this ornament something extra special.

Directions:

1. Poke a hole about one third of the way through the Styrofoam ball with the paintbrush handle. Squeeze glue into the hole.

2. Fold ribbon in half. Poke the ends down into the hole with the paintbrush handle, so that the ribbon forms a loop.

3. Glue shells and beads all over the Styrofoam ball. Let dry, and hang.

Supplies:

Paintbrush
Small Styrofoam ball
Glue
6-inch piece of ribbon
Small shells
Pearly beads

Seashell Friends

These clammy critters will bring you out of your shell!

Directions:

1. Squeeze glue inside a seashell. Push in a pom-pom.

2. Glue googly eyes on the pom-pom. Peekaboo!

Supplies:
Craft glue
Small seashells
Pom-poms
Googly eyes

Rainbow Streamer

Make a colorful rainbow to brighten your day, just as King Triton did at Ariel's wedding!

Directions:

1. Cut 16 pieces of ribbon, each 12 inches long.

2. Put double-sided tape around the inside and the outside of the hoop.

3. Stick one end of a piece of ribbon inside the hoop and wrap it around the hoop to the outside, pressing it onto the tape. Let the other end of the ribbon dangle. Repeat with the other pieces of ribbon. Stick the ribbons close together.

4. Cut three pieces of string, each about 18 inches long. Tie the end of each piece of string to the hoop, evenly spaced.

5. Tie the other ends of the string together in a knot at the top. Hang your rainbow decoration anywhere you need a little color!

Supplies:
Several colors of ribbon

Measuring tape

Scissors

Double-sided tape

3-inch wide hoop
(a wood embroidery
hoop works well)

String

Aurora

Royal Princess Hat

Here's a regal hat perfect for a princess like you!

Directions:

1. Cut the craft foam into a large half circle, about 15 inches across. Curl it into a cone to fit the top of your head, leaving a small hole at the top. Staple in place.

2. Starting at the top, squeeze glue in a spiral pattern, using a continuous line, to the bottom. Press the cord into the glue.

3. Thread one end of the sheer fabric into the top of the hat and staple in place.

Supplies:

Large sheet of colored craft foam

Scissors

Stapler

Craft glue

Shiny cord

Sheer fabric, about 10 inches wide
and one yard long

Bold Banner

Make a colorful flag like the ones the people carried during the celebration of Aurora's birth.

Directions:

1. Thread a long piece of yarn through the straw. Tie the ends together.

2. Cut a felt flag so that it is almost as wide as the length of the straw. Wrap the top of the flag around the straw and glue in place. Let dry.

3. Cut out designs in different colors of felt and glue to the flag. Hang with pride!

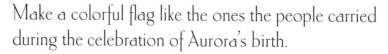

Fancy Fairies

Flora, Fauna, and Merryweather watched over Aurora for nearly sixteen years. Put these little fairies somewhere to keep a watchful eye on you.

Directions:

1. Cut a half circle, about 2 inches across, out of the paper for the fairy's body. Roll the half circle into a cone and tape in place.

2. Cut three smaller half circles, about 1 inch across, and form them into cones for the arms and hat. Tape together.

3. Squeeze some glue onto the top of the body cone and stick on a bead for the head. Glue a small piece from a cotton ball onto top of the head to make hair.

4. Glue the hat on the head. Glue the arms to the sides of the body. Let dry.

5. Squeeze some glue around the bottom edge of the skirt. Sprinkle on some glitter. Draw a happy face on the bead.

Supplies:

Colored paper

Scissors

Tape

Wood beads

Glue

Cotton balls

Glitter

Black pen

Dreamy Dress

The fairies dreamed up a dress fit for a princess for Aurora on her sixteenth birthday. Here's a fun way to create your own princess dress!

Directions:

1.   Cut yourself out of the photocopied picture. Glue onto a piece of white paper.

2.   Cut out a dress from scrap fabric. Glue onto your picture.

3.   Add ribbons, bows, a necklace, and don't forget a crown!

Jeweled Scrapbook

Here's a miniature book worthy of a princess's story!

Directions:

1. Cut two short pieces of ribbon. Glue one across the front of the hinge and one across the back so you can tie the ends in a bow when the hinge is closed.

2. Cut pieces of colored paper to fit the front and back of the hinge. Glue the paper over the ribbon.

3. Decorate the front cover with rhinestones.

4. Cut a long strip of white paper. Fan-fold it to fit inside the hinge. Glue the ends of the paper inside the hinge to make pages.

Berry Patch

Supplies:

Purple and green polymer clay

Toothpick

Aluminum foil

Baking sheet

Make a batch of berries like the ones Aurora went out to pick on her sixteenth birthday— the day she met her prince!

Directions:

1. Make a small oval of purple clay.

2. Roll enough tiny balls of purple clay to cover the oval completely. Press them into place.

3. Roll small green balls and flatten them for leaves. Draw veins with a toothpick.

4. Put foil on a baking sheet and place berries on foil. Bake according to clay package directions. Let cool completely.

Birthday Sweets

Bake a cake like the one Flora, Fauna, and Merryweather made for Aurora, but remember—it may look tasty, but this cake's not for eating!

Supplies:

Brown, white, pink, and green polymer clay

Aluminum foil

Baking sheet

Directions:

1. Roll three equal balls of brown clay about the size of marbles, then flatten them to make the cake layers. Wash the brown clay off your hands.

2. Flatten three pieces of white clay to make frosting. Press the frosting onto each cake layer. Stack the layers.

3. Flatten tiny pink balls and roll them up to make roses. Press onto the top of the cake. Make a few green leaves and press them on.

4. Put foil on the baking sheet and place the cake on the foil. Bake according to clay package directions. Let cool completely.

Snow White

Pebble Turtles

Snow White's turtle friend was always left behind. Don't leave behind these tiny turtles!

Directions:

1. Paint a pebble to look like a turtle shell. Let dry.

2. Cut out a turtle body from construction paper. Glue the pebble to the body.

3. Draw on eyes with the marker.

Supplies:

Pebble
(for each turtle)

Acrylic paint

Paintbrush

Construction paper

Scissors

Craft glue

Black marker

Supplies:

Pipe cleaners

Paintbrush

Fingernail clippers

Large craft feathers

Craft glue

Fluttery Butterflies

These feather-light butterflies are like the ones that flew around in the forest by the Seven Dwarfs' cottage.

Directions:

1. Coil a pipe cleaner around a paintbrush handle to make the body. Slide off.

2. Clip another pipe cleaner in half with the fingernail clippers. Bend one half into a V shape and coil the ends down to make antennae. Poke the V into the coiled butterfly body so the antennae stick out of the top.

3. Put some glue on the ends of the craft feathers and stick them into the body coils for wings.

Baby Birdies

The forest animals and birds kept Snow White company while the Seven Dwarfs were away at the diamond mine. Here's how to hatch a batch of birdies to keep you company.

Directions:

1. Ask an adult to carefully crack open an egg for you. Wash the eggshell carefully and let it dry out.

2. Glue the googly eyes on the large pom-pom. Glue the yellow pom-pom on for a beak. Let dry.

3. Squeeze some glue in the bottom of the eggshell and stick in the large pom-pom. Glue the top of the shell onto the bird's head. "Cheep!"

Supplies:

Eggshell
(for each birdie)

Googly eyes

Craft glue

Large pom-pom

Small yellow pom-pom

Dwarf Dolls

The Seven Dwarfs all loved Snow White—even Grumpy.

Directions:

1. Glue the bead to the cork. Glue on the eyes and the pom-pom for the nose.

2. Clip the pipe cleaner into four parts with the fingernail clippers. Curl the ends for hands and feet. Stick the other ends into the cork.

3. Pull apart a cotton ball and make a beard and hair. Glue to head and face. Don't forget that Dopey doesn't have hair or a beard!

4. Cut a half-circle of felt for the hat. Roll into a cone shape and glue. Hold it together a few minutes until it sticks. Put a little glue around the edges and stick to the head. Heigh-ho!

Supplies:

(for each doll)

Wooden bead

Cork

Googly eyes

Tiny pom-pom

Craft glue

Pipe cleaner

Fingernail clippers

Cotton ball

Felt

Scissors

Supplies:

Small box with lid

Fabric paint

Glue

Felt

Scissors

Bitty Beds

Each of the Seven Dwarfs has his own bed with his name on it to sleep in at night. Your cork versions of the Seven Dwarfs need a place to sleep, too!

Directions:

1. Take the lid off the box. Turn the box upside down. Fit the lid on the edge of the box to make a headboard.

2. Use fabric paint to write a dwarf's name on the headboard. Let dry.

3. Cut a felt rectangle for a blanket. Roll up a strip of felt for a pillow and glue ends together. Sweet dreams!

Sweety Pie

When the Seven Dwarfs found out Snow White could make gooseberry pie, they were certain she should stay!

Directions:

1. Mold a small piece of aluminum foil into a tiny pie plate.

2. Roll out a circle of tan clay and line the pie plate with it. Crimp the edges of the crust with the end of a toothpick.

3. Make tiny balls of red clay to make berries, and fill the crust full. Wash the red clay off your hands.

4. Make two tiny hearts out of tan clay and press in place on top of the berries.

5. Bake the pie according to the clay package directions. Let cool completely. This is a treat that you can't eat, but you can treasure.

Supplies:

Aluminum foil

Tan and red polymer clay

Roller (a glass or jar works well)

Butter knife

Toothpick

Baking sheet

Blossom Pots

When Snow White cleaned the Seven Dwarfs' cottage, she put fresh flowers on the table. These flower place holders will freshen your table!

Directions:

1. Press a piece of foam into each pot. Stick the end of a pipe cleaner in the foam. Add a pipe cleaner leaf at the base. Cover the foam with the moss.

2. Coil down the other end of the pipe cleaner.

3. Cut out a flower shape from the construction paper and write on a name with a marker.

4. Stick the flower into the coil of the pipe cleaner. Now it's time to set the table.

Belle

Royal Crown

When Belle marries her prince and lives in the castle, she'll wear a crown like this one.

Directions:

1. Ask an adult to cut a crown shape out of the soda bottle with the craft knife.

2. Decorate with glitter glue. Glue on some rhinestones for sparkle. Let dry and wear. You may need bobby pins to secure to your head. Or you can cut open the back and wear as a sparkling tiara.

Supplies:

Empty 2-liter soda bottle

Craft knife

Glitter glue

Flat-backed
rhinestones

Tweet-Tweet Treat

Belle and the Beast fed the birds at the castle during the winter. With this easy bird feeder, you can help the birds at your castle!

Directions:

1. Cut one of the plastic plates in half. Staple one half of the plate to the whole plate, so it forms a pocket for the birdseed.

2. Decorate the feeder with fabric paint. Let dry.

3. Punch two holes at the top of the feeder and tie on a piece of string to make a hanger.

4. Fill the pocket with birdseed. Hang the feeder outside for your feathered friends.

Enchanted Rose

The Beast earned Belle's love before the last petal of his enchanted rose fell—and he turned into a handsome prince!

Directions:

1. Fill a paper cup half full with water and add five drops of food coloring.

2. Fold each of the coffee filters in fourths and dip each into the colored water. Lay them flat on the newspaper to dry.

3. Stack the dry filters on top of each other. Punch two holes in the middle, about an inch apart.

4. Thread the end of the pipe cleaner up through one hole and down through the other. Twist the end of the pipe cleaner to itself to secure in place and bend the middle into a leaf.

5. Scrunch up the filters in the middle to make the rose. If you would like your rose to smell sweet, ask an adult if you can spray it with a little perfume.

Supplies:

Paper cup
Red food coloring
Seven coffee filters
Newspaper
Hole punch
Green pipe cleaner

Magical Mirror

The Beast gave Belle a magical mirror as something to always remember him by. Here's a way to add some of your own magic to a plain hand mirror.

Directions:

1. Place the mirror on a sheet of newspaper. Spread a thick coat of glue all around the edge of the mirror.

2. Working quickly, sprinkle on seed beads, then sprinkle on fine glitter to fill in the gaps. Let dry.

3. Shake off excess glitter. Smile!

Supplies:
Hand mirror
Newspaper
Craft glue
Seed (tiny) beads
Glitter or microbeads

Supplies:

Cardboard box

4 toilet-paper tubes

Craft foam or
construction paper

Scissors

Tape

Glue

Toothpicks

Markers

Grand Castle

After the Beast's spell was broken, his gloomy home turned
into a beautiful castle!

Directions:

1. Cover box and tubes with craft foam or construction paper and tape in place.
Tape tubes to each corner of box.

2. Make cones to tape on top of the turrets and glue on toothpick flags.

3. Cut windows and doors out of paper, glue in place, and move in!

Jasmine

Treasure Box

Only one worthy person could enter the treasure-filled Cave of Wonders—Aladdin. Here's a box worthy of your own treasures!

Directions:

1. Paint the box with acrylic paint. Let dry.

2. Draw designs on the box with glitter glue.

3. Stick on rhinestones with glue.

4. Let box dry completely, and then store your treasures!

Supplies:

Plain wood or cardboard box

Acrylic paint

Paintbrush

Glitter glue

Flat-backed rhinestones

55

Dazzling Bottles

There were all sorts of wonderful jars and bottles at the Agrabah market. Here's how to make a few of your own.

Directions:

1. Wash and dry the bottle and remove the label.

2. Tear the tissue or foil wrappers into small pieces.

3. Paint glue onto a small part of the bottle. Cover the glue with pieces of tissue or foil wrappers, overlapping the pieces. Cover the whole bottle, then let dry.

Funny Monkey

This mischievous monkey is like Abu—always up to something!

Directions:

1. Glue the two pom-poms together to make a body and head.

2. Cut ears and a face out of the tan felt and glue in place. Glue on googly eyes. Draw mouth.

3. Clip a pipe cleaner into four pieces with the fingernail clippers. Bend two pieces into legs and two pieces into arms. Glue in place.

4. Cut another pipe cleaner in half. Bend one half into a tail and glue in place. Let dry and then have fun monkeying around.

Supplies:

1 large and 1 medium brown pom-pom

Craft glue

Tan felt

Scissors

Black marker

Brown pipe cleaners

Fingernail clippers

Googly eyes

Terrrr-ific Tiger Pencil Holder

Jasmine's best friend was Rajah, her tiger.
This easy-to-make pencil holder is a great gift
for your best friend.

Directions:

1. Look for preprinted striped foam at the craft store. If you can't find it, make your own! Use a permanent marker to color tiger stripes on plain orange craft foam. (Be careful not to get any marker on your clothes.)

2. Cut a piece of foam to fit around the juice can. Glue in place. Wrap a few rubber bands around the can to hold the foam in place while it dries. Cut cord to fit around top and bottom of can. Glue in place. Let dry. Grrrrowl!

Supplies:
Tiger-striped craft foam
Scissors
Empty juice can
Glue
Rubber bands
Cord

Hidden Treasure

Aladdin and Abu discovered countless treasures in the Cave of Wonders.

Directions:

1. Remove label from bottle. Fill the bottle about one third full of sand.

2. Add a few tablespoons of glitter and the treasures. Tighten the lid. Roll the bottle to uncover treasures in the sand.

Supplies:

Empty small plastic soda bottle

Sand

Glitter

Small treasures like beads, marbles, or rhinestones

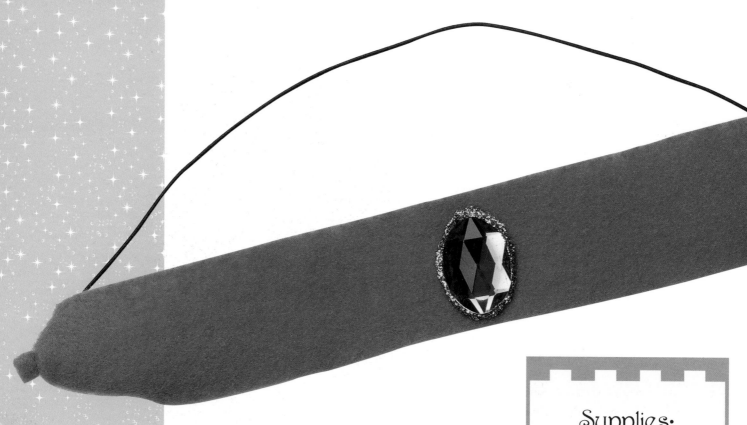

Jeweled Headband

Make a headband just like Jasmine's!

Directions:

1. Cut a headband about 8 inches long and 1 ½ inches wide out of the felt.

2. Squeeze a large blob of fabric paint or glitter glue in the middle of the headband. Press the rhinestone into the paint or glue. Let dry.

3. Cut a piece of elastic 6 inches long. Tie each end onto the ends of the headband. Slip over your head with the elastic in back and wear like a princess!

Starry-Night Frame

Jasmine will never forget the night Aladdin took her flying on the Magic Carpet through the starry night. Put a picture of your own favorite memory in this starry-night frame.

Directions:

1. Paint the frame black. Let dry completely.

2. Draw stars on the frame with the gel pen. Now just add a picture!

Supplies:

Plain wood or cardboard
picture frame

Black acrylic paint

Paintbrush

White opaque gel pen